Grey Rabbit's May Day

Alison Uttley
pictures by Margaret Tempest

Collins

William Collins Sons & Co Ltd
London · Glasgow · Sydney · Auckland
Toronto · Johannesburg

First published 1963
© text The Alison Uttley Literary Property Trust 1987
© illustrations The Estate of Margaret Tempest 1987
© this arrangement William Collins Sons & Co Ltd 1987
Second impression 1988

Cover decoration by Fiona Owen
Decorated capital by Mary Cooper
Alison Uttley's original story has been abridged for this book.
Uttley, Alison
Little Grey Rabbit's May day. —
Rev. ed — (Little Grey Rabbit books)
I. Title   II. Tempest, Margaret
II. Series
823'.912[J]   PZ10.3

ISBN 0-00-194226-3

Typeset by Columns of Reading
Made and printed in Great Britain by
William Collins Sons and Co Ltd, Glasgow

FOREWORD

Of course you must understand that Grey Rabbit's home had no electric light or gas, and even the candles were made from pith of rushes dipped in wax from the wild bees' nests, which Squirrel found. Water there was in plenty, but it did not come from a tap. It flowed from a spring outside, which rose up from the ground and went to a brook. Grey Rabbit cooked on a fire, but it was a wood fire, there was no coal in that part of the country. Tea did not come from India, but from a little herb known very well to country people, who once dried it and used it in their cottage homes. Bread was baked from wheat ears, ground fine, and Hare and Grey Rabbit gleaned in the cornfields to get the wheat.

The doormats were plaited rushes, like country-made mats, and cushions were stuffed with wool gathered from the hedges where sheep pushed through the thorns. As for the looking-glass, Grey Rabbit found the glass, dropped from a lady's handbag, and Mole made a frame for it. Usually the animals gazed at themselves in the still pools as so many country children have done. The country ways of Grey Rabbit were the country ways known to the author.

The wild winds of March had died away, April had come with sweet-tasting rain and tender grasses and the Cuckoo's call. Now May was near and every little creature rejoices when it is Maytime.

"It's May Day tomorrow," announced Hare at breakfast time one morning. "There's going to be dancing round the Maypole in the village. The Maypole is set up ready with fine ribbons hanging down and the children will dance like me. I danced round last night when the children had gone to bed, so there!"

"Hare! Did you? In the moonlight?" cried Grey Rabbit, astonished.

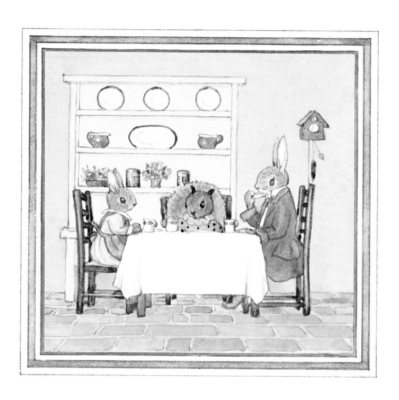

"Yes," laughed Hare. "I tried to bring you a ribbon but they were fastened out of my reach. I jigged till I heard the policeman's heavy tread and then I scampered away."

"Could we have a Maypole?" asked Squirrel. "I want to dance round it and I'm afraid to go to the village."

"We'll dance round the May tree and that's better than a Maypole," said Grey Rabbit. "There's a lovely May tree in the field with blossom coming out."

"Let's have a procession like the children," said Hare, leaping up with excitement. "They sing a carol and carry crowns and sceptres."

"Let me think," implored Grey Rabbit. And she put her paw to her head and stood very still.

"I'll think too," said Squirrel, imitating her and standing very still, too.

"I can think without this fuss," said Hare, scornfully.

"We must gather lots of flowers with May-dew on their petals on May morning," said Grey Rabbit. "I'll take a jug to catch some May-dew, for it's magical. We must make crowns and garlands for May. I think I must ask Wise Owl about all this."

So away they went after the breakfast things were washed to find Wise Owl.

On the way Hedgehog and Moldy Warp joined them.

"May Day?" asked Wise Owl, sleepily, looking down at the company. "How to keep May Day? May is the Queen of the flowers. You must make crowns and sceptres for her. She's invisible, but you hang them on a May tree and she will find them."

"It's in my Book of Wisdom," went on the great bird. He brought out the green book. "Make a crown of flowers and a sceptre and cowslip balls. Take them to a May tree," he read slowly, spectacles on beak.

"What kind of flowers, Wise Owl?" called Hare.

"It says 'Cowslips and all Spring flowers but at the top of the crown there must be a Crown Imperial'," Wise Owl answered.

"I've never heard of a Crown Imperial. What is it?" they said.

Moldy Warp spoke up. "I once saw a fine flower in the garden of the Big House," said he. "I saw the Crown Imperial. I heard the head-gardener tell the under-gardeners there was a pearl in each lily bell, like a tear."

"What was it like?" asked Grey Rabbit.

"It was like a ring of golden bells with a green topknot of leaves," said the Mole. "I sat underneath it."

"Then I've seen it in the village," said Old Hedgehog slowly. "Sometimes there are orange bells, Mr Moldy Warp."

Moldy Warp frowned. "The Crown Imperial is a noble lily and it lives in grand gardens," said he.

"In cottage gardens, too," said Hedgehog. "I've seen it in Miss Susan's border."

Hare leapt up. He sprang so high that Wise Owl shook his head at him and ruffled his feathers.

"I've seen it too," he shouted. So Wise Owl turned his back and returned to the tree.

"Noisy crowd, always argy-bargying," he murmured.

"It grows in her border," cried Hare. "Miss Susan taught me to make lace. I was looking out of the corner of my eye and I saw a tall yellow lily."

"You'd better get one from the Old Lady," said Hedgehog.

"Yes, I will," said Hare.

"What can I do?" asked Fuzzypeg, who joined his father on the way home.

"You can make cowslip balls, Fuzzypeg. You know where cowslips grow, and you are a good ball-maker," said Grey Rabbit.

"Let me make a sceptre," called little voices from all over the place, as heads popped from holes and tree trunks and rocky shelters.

"Yes, all of you can make sceptres on May morning," said Grey Rabbit and they hurried back home.

On May morning a company of small animals came from their cottages and ran to the fields and hedgebanks to gather fresh flowers with dew on the petals. Grey Rabbit carried a tiny jug for May-dew and Squirrel had a basket for flowers, but Hare was impatient to discover the Crown Imperials.

Moldy Warp went to a willow by the stream and began to cut withies with his little axe. Then Grey Rabbit, Squirrel and Hare came up.

"A happy May Day," they called. "Why are you getting withies?"

"Why? Because you must have a foundation for the crowns and garlands," said he, scornfully, and he stripped off the tender leaves and twined the slender withies to make hoops and rings.

"You fasten the flowers to these," he explained.

"I'm going to the village to get the Crown Imperials from Miss Susan's garden," said Hare, as he impatiently twisted the willow and tied a few bunches of flowers to the framework.

"You can't just go and take Miss Susan's precious flowers without asking," objected Grey Rabbit.

"Give her a cowslip ball," suggested Squirrel.

Little Fuzzypeg was sitting near them with a basket of cowslips. He was busy threading the golden heads on a string of plaited grasses. By his side lay two beautiful cowslip balls, even and round.

"Can I have one for Miss Susan?" asked Grey Rabbit, stooping to admire his work. She picked up a ball and smelled its honey scent and tossed it and caught it.

"Yes, Grey Rabbit dear," said the little Hedgehog. "I like Miss Susan. She is kind to little animals."

"I've got a hanky made of cobweb," said Grey Rabbit, putting her paw in her pocket. "I'll send that too."

"I've got a walnut shell with nothing in it," said Squirrel, and she held out an empty shell.

"Fill it with new-mown hay," said Grey Rabbit. So Squirrel picked some of the white starry flowers of wood-ruff, which have the smell of fresh hay, and filled the little box. She tied the walnut's lid with green grasses, and it made a scent-box for Miss Susan.

"I've got something at home for the Old Lady," said Moldy Warp. "I'll go back to my cupboard where I keep my bits and bobs of findings. I've cut enough withies for you now."

Hare scampered along by the side of the slow-plodding Mole.

"Not much time to waste," said he as he leapt round his friend, urging him on. "I must get those Crown Imperials before even the blacksmith wakes up. Nobody must see me."

"I won't be long," said Mole.

Moldy Warp unlocked his door and disappeared in his dark house. He went to the cupboard in the earthy wall. Some of Badger's findings from deep underground were there, and his own ancestral collection of treasure.

"I could give her an arrow-head," he pondered, stroking a grey stone, "or a Roman penny, or this bone pin carved with a hare at the end, or a jet ring – yet it might not fit her."

Then he pounced on something and took it to the light. It was a tiny bottle only two inches long, green as grass, square and squat.

"This'll do. I'll fill it with dew from Grey Rabbit's jug, and it will make her young again."

Then he took the carved bone pin and put it with the bottle.

"Hullo, Moldy Warp. I thought you were going to stay all day," said Hare crossly. "What have you got? A dirty little green bottle and an old bone pin with me on the top?"

"Never you mind," said Moldy Warp, and he trotted back twice as fast, eager to show his finds to the company. The animals left their crowns and sceptres to look.

"Here's a Roman bottle they kept their tears in," said he.

"I'm sure Miss Susan doesn't cry," protested Hare.

"We are going to put some of Grey Rabbit's May-dew into it," said Moldy Warp.

"Yes, I gathered it from the May-blossom as soon as the sun's rays shone on it. It's magical," said Grey Rabbit.

"If Miss Susan puts a drop on her eyes she will see more clearly," said Moldy Warp. "A drop on her cheeks will make the wrinkles vanish, and a drop on her crooked fingers will give her new strength."

So very carefully Moldy Warp filled the tiny green bottle from Grey Rabbit's jug of May-dew and Hare stuffed a wad of hawthorn in the top for a cork.

"Sorry I was cross, Moldy Warp," he muttered.

"That's all right," said Moldy Warp kindly as he held up the bone pin. "It's a Roman pin to fasten up her dress," said he.

"She can use it for a lace-bobbin," said Hare. "It's just like the bobbins that hang from her lace pillow. Thank you very much, Moldy Warp."

"Now go off, Hare, and take all these presents and the cowslip ball. Miss Susan will gladly give you a Crown Imperial," they told him, and away he galloped, his big pockets full and the cowslip ball dangling on his arm.

But Hare was late. The children, too, had been up at dawn, putting the finishing touches on their crowns and sceptres ready for the procession.

Hare could see boys and girls having breakfast, while the garlands lay in the cool shadows outside.

In every crown sat a little doll, and at the top of each crown was a fine Crown Imperial.

"I hope they've left me one or two," he muttered as he dashed down the road towards Miss Susan's cottage.

Yes, there under the wall of the cottage was a row of fine golden flowers, each with five bells and a green topknot. Yellow Brimstones flew among them and bumble-bees sipped the honey.

"Please, Miss Susan!" cried Hare, as he banged on the door with his furry fists. Nobody answered. Miss Susan was not well, she lay in her bed, half-dreaming.

"A happy May Day," squeaked Hare through the key-hole.

"Same to you," murmured Miss Susan. Then she started. "Who can it be? A mouse?" she asked herself. "Is it one of the children? Do they want some Crown Imperials for their May Day? Here I lie, and once I was Queen of the May. Now I can't even get up on May morning."

She listened, but there was no patter of feet, only a rustle as Hare slipped among the tall lilies.

"Who's there?" she called.

"It's only Hare. I wanted something," squeaked Hare, but she could not hear his high voice. Hare cut two lilies, panting as he bit through the thick stalks, looking around nervously as footsteps came near.

"He went in here! He's gone somewhere about here!" said a boy's voice.

Hare hurriedly dropped his presents where the Crown Imperials had grown – the tiny Roman tear bottle filled with the dew of May, the Roman pin with a hare on the top, the walnut shell stuffed with new-mown hay, the little lace handkerchief – but the cowslip ball he hung on the door knob. Then, clutching the golden flowers he leapt down the steps and away.

"After him! Catch him! A hare's been taking Miss Susan's lilies," the children cried as they tore after him. But nobody can catch a hare at full gallop, and Hare got safely away.

Later on the procession was formed. The children carried their heavy crowns on sticks threaded through the back of the flowery burdens. Auriculas and primulas, cowslips and bluebells covered the wicker frames, and at the tip of each crown and sceptre was a noble Crown Imperial. Inside the crown sat a small doll with a veil, for that is the old custom. The children went from the school to the village green and they sang the May Day carol.

Miss Susan dressed slowly and looked out at the children as they passed her door.

"Miss Susan, Miss Susan," they called. "There was a hare in your garden this morning, early. He took your Crown Imperials."

"Whatever did he want with my flowers?" wavered Miss Susan sadly. "I wish they had gone to make a crown," she said, and she turned away. Then she stopped for she saw the cowslip ball hanging on the door knob.

Then something among the lily leaves caught her eye. She picked up the walnut and inside were the flowers of new-mown hay. She found the wee small handkerchief of cobweb and the bone carved pin with the hare on the top. She stooped down and picked up the little green bottle of ancient glass. She sniffed at it and poured a drop on her hands. "Nice smell," said she. She tasted it and rubbed a little on her aching head and eyes. Her headache vanished, her eyes sparkled, her face was fresh and young again.

"This pin will make a lace-bobbin. Where did these things come from? This hanky is a fairy thing."

Then she remembered the children said a hare had been in the garden.

"Once I taught a hare to make lace. Yes, that's it. On May Day anything might happen."

Away in the pasture another little procession was forming. Grey Rabbit fastened the Crown Imperial to the top of the lovely crown, which was made of cowslips, bluebells, king-cups and forget-me-nots.

"There was a doll in the crown I saw," said Hare.

"Yes, there ought to be a doll by rights," said Moldy Warp. "Who's got a doll?"

They looked at one another.

"I haven't got a doll," said Grey Rabbit. "Nor me. Nor me," said Squirrel and Fuzzypeg.

Then Rat stepped forward from behind a rock where he had been watching.

"I can make a doll for you," said he. "I made one for our baby, out of a bit of bone. I can carve a doll all right."

He picked up a bit of oak and shaped it with his teeth so that there appeared a pretty little figure.

"How clever you are, Rat," said Grey Rabbit.

"Too clever by half," muttered Hare. Nobody had told him he was clever to get the Crown Imperials.

"Hush! That was rude," whispered Grey Rabbit, and she dressed the little doll in a skirt of leaves and made a bodice of cowslips. On its head she put a crown of May-blossom, and in its hand a bluebell wand.

So the flowery doll sat in the middle of the crown, under the great Crown Imperial.

Grey Rabbit and Squirrel slung the crown on a hazel stick and carried it between them.

Hare walked in front with a tall Crown Imperial sceptre. Fuzzypeg followed after with two cowslip balls. Then came Mr Hedgehog and Mrs Hedgehog with a smaller crown of May-blossom, and after them Water-rat carrying a water-lily sceptre. Moldy Warp followed with a sceptre of crab-apple blossom, and the little Hedgehogs, Bill and Tim, walked with a garland of May and bluebells.

As they went their winding way to the old twisted hawthorn, the animals sang their own May song. Their tiny voices were mingled with those of the cuckoo calling, the nightingale singing, the robins and wrens, the blackbirds and throstles, all chanting with joy because it was May Day.

"May, May, we sing to the May
To sun and moon and Milky Way,
To field and wood and growing hay,
On the First of May.

Grey Rabbit and Hare, Squirrel and all,
Fuzzypeg with cowslip ball,
We carry the crown for beautiful May,
The sceptres and garlands,
This joyful day.
May Day. The First of May."

They hung the crowns and sceptres on the
May tree, and then they danced around. The
May tree rustled her branches and sent waves
of perfume up to the blue sky, while all the
birds came flying to the tree to join in the
song of welcome to May.

At night, when everybody was fast asleep, Wise Owl flew over the May tree. The tree shone like silver, and in its branches hung the crown of flowers with the Crown Imperial, the sceptres and the cowslip balls.

> "Too whit. Too whoo,
> Happy May Day to you."

called Wise Owl; and then he listened, for he could hear a silvery answer which seemed to come from the tree itself.

"May Day. May Day. May Day," sang the tree and the Wise Owl shivered with delight.